Witches'

Knickers

(and other stories)

A collection of contemporary short

stories by

Angela Wooldridge

CONTENTS

Witches' Knickers

'It's bad enough that my mum's the crazy woman who collects witches' knickers,' Martha heard Zoe complain to her friend. 'But now she's talking about it on local radio!'

'Oh Zoe,' sighed Martha as she left the house. 'You don't know the half of it.'

She chivvied the dog into the car. Why was she doing this? It had started as a crusade, but now it felt like one more rut she couldn't get out of.

'Why carry on then?' Stuart had shrugged. 'No-one's *asking* you to do it.'

She half suspected that if she started pole-dancing in a sleazy dive, Stuart would just shrug and say, 'OK, whatever.'

'For goodness sake,' she wanted to shout at him. 'Engage!'

Was he like this with everyone? He was working late a lot and locked himself away in the shed most evenings. Wasn't that one of those signs you were meant to look out for?

'Don't go there,' she told herself. 'Just… just don't.'

She switched on the radio and set off.

'Today we are talking to Martha Hames. Hello Martha.'

'Hello, Judy.'

Martha winced at how squeaky her voice sounded.

'Now, Martha, you've come to our attention because of a rather unusual pastime; collecting Witches' Knickers.'

'You make it sound a lot more exciting than it really is.'

'Could you explain it to our listeners in your own words?'

'OK, 'witches' knickers' is a rather colourful term used to describe discarded carrier bags that get tangled up in trees and hedges.'

'Litter, in other words.'

'Yep, that's the stuff,' she reached her destination and heaved the car up onto a grassy bank.

'And you collect this litter.'

'Yep.' Martha agreed. She fiddled with her phone. It still amazed her that she could continue listening with a few taps of the screen. Of course, she'd never admit that to Zoe, who was convinced that anyone born in the last century couldn't possibly understand the modern world.

'C'mon Rufus.' The dog jumped from the car as she grabbed a bin liner and litter-picker, and they set to work.

'What inspired you to do this?'

'I'm not sure I remember precisely.'

Actually she could remember all too well. Zoe had been going through a phase of hating everyone, especially Martha. And Stuart seemed oblivious to everything.

'I guess I must have been having a bad day.'

'Understatement,' she snorted.

'A shopping bag broke as I was loading the car. "Right, that's it!" I said. "I don't need their crummy bags."'

'The words I used were a bit stronger than that.'

'"I know where there's a perfectly good bag. It's been there for months!" And I drove off to this bag that had been hanging in the hedge for weeks.'

Judy laughed. *'What happened then?'*

'Standing there, holding that stupid little bag felt like the most successful moment I'd had all day. It was completely useless for shopping, of course, all grey and gritty and horrible. But it was fine for holding the other rubbish strewn around, and that's what I did. I spent half an hour tidying the hedge while the ice-cream melted in the car.'

'Is melted ice-cream an occupational hazard?'

Oh yes. Ice-cream-gate. Anyone would have thought the world had ended.

'The next time I put a bit more thought into it.'

'Have you found anything interesting?'

'I once found an engagement ring.'

She'd recognised Sally Wheeler's ring at once. Sally had burst into tears when she'd returned it. She'd thought that David had been cheating on her, and had been so mad that she'd stopped the car and thrown it as hard and as far as she could.

What if Stuart..? No, don't go there.

'You've been doing this for nearly a year now. I gather you've become part of the local colour and people look out for you.'

'Hmm.'

'Isn't that a good thing?'

'I suppose it would be nice to set an example. But then it's not exactly anyone's career choice, is it?'

'Speaking of careers, you fit this inbetween working and bringing up a family don't you?'

'Yes. I work part-time, and my daughter is still at school.'

'Thank you for coming in, Martha. Keep up the good work! After the break we'll be taking calls from our listeners. What do you think about Martha's activities? We'd love to hear from you.'

The interview had been recorded yesterday. Then she'd felt fine about it, but now she wasn't sure she was ready to listen to the phone-in.

'She's crazy. If she wants to walk the dog, why not go to the park like everyone else?'

'There must be a health and safety issue here. She should leave it to the people whose job it is.'

'But it doesn't seem to be anyone's job.'

'Then it's an opportunity to create work, and she's taking that away from someone who needs it.'

'I think she's great. There should be more out there like her.'

'Does she use any special kit?'

Martha switched off in disgust.

'Great, I'm an embarrassment to my daughter, my husband might be having an affair, and everyone else thinks I'm crazy.' She stabbed at the hedge, her mouth twisting with the effort of holding back her sobs.

'There she is!'

'Hello! Excuse me!'

'Mrs uh... *what's she called?'*

*'Martha...*Martha! Yoo-hoo'

Oh no, now what?

She wiped her face on her sleeve, and turned.

Three young women were hopping out of a car.

'We heard you on the radio.'

'We've been looking all over for you.'

'Can we help?'

They looked keen, fresh and held bin liners. Two more cars drew up.

'There she is!'

'Let's start over here.'

'…we thought; why hasn't anyone else done this?'

'…great community spirit.'

'… you must be so proud…'

'…said it's about time we showed some support.'

'…that last call…'

'…so here we are!'

She looked at the crowd of eager helpers and struggled to think of something to say. Then a figure emerged from a familiar looking car with something strapped to its back. She blinked hard, but it still looked like Stuart. What was he doing here, and what *was* that?

He made his way through the crowd, ignoring Rufus who jumped excitedly up at him and came to stand before her.

'It's for sorting the litter.' Stuart jerked his head at the thing on his back. 'I've been making it in the shed. See, this section is for plastics, this is for anything non-recyclable. There's a compartment here for anything interesting, a slot for hand gel, and watch this! It crushes cans.'

The thin veneer of doubt over Martha's heart cracked. She gave a shaky laugh and smiled mistily at him.

He shrugged. 'Well, considering what Zoe said on the radio, I'm glad I made it.'

'Zoe?'

'Surely you heard?'

'It was the last call!'

'You can't have missed it!'

'Here…' One of the women tapped the screen of her phone a few times and held it up for everyone to hear.

'…*one last call. This is Zoe, from Exeter.*'

'*My name is Zoe Hames. I just want to say; that's my mum you're talking about. I think she's brilliant and I'm really proud of what she's done.*'

Martha burst into tears and threw her arms around Stuart.

The helpers drew back and left them alone.

'If you don't like it,' Stuart was saying anxiously, 'I can take it off.'

'You leave it right there,' she told him. 'That contraption tells me you love me more than any stupid old ring could.'

'What *are* you talking about?'

'I thought… you've been working so late,' she sniffed. 'When you are home, we barely talk. I was afraid that you weren't happy any more.'

Stuart produced a hankie and shook her affectionately. 'I've arranged with work to stay late some nights so that I can take an afternoon off a week to help you.'

She looked at her new workforce. They were desperately scratching around for some speck of rubbish from the area she'd spent the last half hour clearing.

'With all this new help, I could take an afternoon off to take on Zoe,' she said.

Stuart wrapped an arm round her, 'You might need two for that.' He watched the small crowd. 'D'you think they'll start polishing the grass soon?'

Martha giggled. She knew just what she wanted to do with her unexpectedly free afternoon.

First published in *My Weekly* June 2017.

This is a favourite of mine. It got turned down by all the mags, but Karen Byron, the fiction editor at *My Weekly,* gave it a second chance if I'd edit it to match the My Weekly word count. It was a better story after the trim too.

That summer, I attended a workshop by Karen at Sidmouth Literary Festival, and she used this as one of her example stories!

BLIND DATE

I'm just like Velma in Scooby-doo. I can't see a thing without my glasses. I never expected that to be so useful on a blind date.

The cafe was a bright oasis of warmth. Thank goodness I'd picked somewhere familiar. My date hadn't seemed keen when I'd suggested it, but now I knew I could make it there blindfolded.

I pushed back my hood, blinked the raindrops from my lashes and shrugged philosophically. Even if I'd been wearing my glasses they'd have steamed up coming in from the cold. I straightened my shoulders and counted the tables from the door.

'You must be Matt!' I was nervous and late, which made me come across as super-cheery to make up for it.

The man-shaped blur glanced up in surprise from putting his coat on. 'Actually, I'm—'

I thrust my hand forward. It had been a rotten evening so far, and I was determined that this date wasn't going to be another failure to add to the list. 'I'm Molly. So sorry I'm late. The underground was chaos, and to top it all someone just crashed into me and knocked my glasses flying.'

They'd been my best pair that framed my eyes nicely, and whoever-it-was had barely noticed me in a tangle at his feet, let alone the glasses catapulting through the air. Despite the busy street, I swear I'd heard them crunch beneath the tyres of a black cab.

'I think—'

He still looked ready to leave, so I rushed on, 'Fortunately I'd memorised what table you said you were seated at. Fourth one along.' I beamed at him.

'Thank you so much for that, otherwise we'd be in a right mess.'

His attention drifted past my shoulder to the other side of the cafe, and I held my breath. Had my stream of chatter scared him off? Or was there someone better looking and less flustered over there he'd been about to chat up? I blinked myopically in the same direction, but it was all just a big colourful blur.

'My friends call me Rob.' He turned back to me, shrugging his jacket back off and I breathed a sigh of relief. 'So Molly, what would you like to drink?'

Silly really, I reflected as I sat down. I wouldn't have been so determined to continue the date if it hadn't been such a performance to get here, especially as he'd seemed a bit full of himself in his messages.

I rummaged in my bag as he gave our order, and triumphantly unearthed my spare glasses. My friend, Diana, called them my 'science nerd specs', but I hadn't a hope of seeing the specials board without them.

My date, now that he was in focus, had the slightly scruffy, roguish charm that Diana and I often drooled over in movies, and I silently thanked whoever had bumped into me. I'd never have had the guts to approach him if I'd seen him first. I crossed my fingers and hoped he wasn't all surface.

My phone pinged imperiously. 'Oh, I'm sorry,' I said. 'I missed a couple of messages from you.' My eyes widened as I took in what they said, and I looked back at Matt... Rob... whatever he wanted to call himself, in disappointment. It looked like I'd been right after all.

It was a shame because he had a wicked smile that was currently directed at the other side of the room again.

'I love that you wear glasses,' he said. 'And even more that you lost them.'

Puzzled, I followed his gaze to the fourth table from the *other* side of the door.

The too-smooth good looks of the man just leaving were spoiled by his sulky expression as he thrust his phone into his pocket and tossed a bunch of convenience store carnations in the bin.

My mouth formed a perfect 'O' as I turned back to my… my… not-my-date-after-all.

'Did you want the flowers?' he asked contritely.

I shook my head slowly.

'Good.' He grinned again as our waitress set our drinks in front of us. 'So, Molly, tell me about your day.'

First published in *My Weekly* March 2020.

This started life as a homework piece for my writing group (we set a homework prompt for each meeting - sometimes I even do it!) The prompt was 'glasses', and being extremely short-sighted has given me endless situations of saying hello to the wrong people.

NOT JUST FOR CHRISTMAS

'Now, this is not just for Christmas, Izzy,' cautioned Aunt May. 'It's for your birthday too.'

At age twenty-five that was just as annoying as it had been at five, ten and fifteen.

Years ago, Mum had explained to family members how upsetting it was for me to have my birthday and Christmas gifts lumped together, whilst watching my summer born brother and sister celebrate completely separate events.

Aunt May had stuck with this for a couple of years before quietly ignoring the request.

'Go ahead and open it,' she urged now.

'Oh, but—'

'I know it's not your birthday until tomorrow, but we don't need to stand on ceremony.'

Gingerly I began to peel off the wrappings. Aunt May always *meant* well, but she had a dreadful habit of buying for herself without thinking too much about who the gift was for.

'These are all the rage right now,' she chirped. 'I had to queue outside the shop for ages.'

My heart sank. No matter how awful it was, I would have to look pleased. The trick would be not to overdo it, else she'd give me the same thing next year.

'How lovely.' The label on the box told me all I needed to know. *Magic Beads* had taken our local high street by storm last year. Each handcrafted bead held a different meaning, and you could make your own selection to thread onto a bracelet or necklace. I could picture Aunt May looking in the window and working out who she could justify buying them for.

'There, I knew it.' She pulled the bracelet from the box and draped it across my wrist. '*So* you.'

I smiled dutifully and thanked her.

The next day was Christmas Eve and my birthday. I was determined to get into town early so I wouldn't need to queue down the street from *Magic Beads* to refund my bracelet.

I knew it seemed mean, but they really weren't my style. Mum had brought me up to be polite and always say thank you for any gifts. No matter how much I disliked something, she'd said, I should be grateful they'd given me anything, and to think about how hurtful it might be to have it rejected. But when I'd had a clear-out a few years back, the small mountain of unused items had convinced me that I didn't have to keep everything either.

My day didn't quite work out as simply as I'd planned though.

Firstly, my mum and sister swept me off for a morning at the local spa.

Now this was a gift I had no intention of turning down, and the facial, massage and catch up with Mum and Emily left me feeling refreshed and at peace with the world. Even with Aunt May, although not enough to keep the bracelet.

Then Dad and my brother met us for lunch.

'But I'm supposed to be meeting Sally in town,' I protested.

'Don't worry, we'll get you there,' Dad smiled. 'Splendid idea, this. Aidan and I got a game of golf in while you were being pampered. Your birthday is such an ideal time to get everyone together.'

'Families are supposed to get together at Christmas,' I said.

'But this is your birthday!' they all chorused.

I looked away, grinning. At least my nearest and dearest had it right.

'I'm very sorry, sir,' the receptionist was saying to a beanpole of a man nearby. 'The last table has just been taken by a birthday party.'

'But you said I didn't need to book!'

'I'm very sorry, sir.' The receptionist didn't look it, and I belatedly realised that it was my group that had taken his table.

'Never mind,' he sighed irritably. 'Perhaps someone could paint my grandmother's toenails so that she, at least, gets something out of this trip?'

Lunch was perfect; beef and ale pie with chips and not a turkey or mince pie in sight. My brother grudgingly agreed to give me a lift afterwards, even though he didn't really feel like moving.

'Better yet, here's a taxi,' he said as we got outside.

The driver lowered his window. 'Taxi for—?'

'Yes, just for one. Here, my treat. Happy birthday, Sis!' Aidan bundled me into the back.

As we drove away, I caught sight of the man I'd seen earlier, his tall figure dwarfing the sprightly elder woman beside him. He looked as if he were trying to flag us down, but we'd rounded the bend before I could tell for sure.

Town brought me closer to *Magic Beads*, but it remained just out of reach as Sally insisted on treating me to a movie and we managed to snag the last two seats.

'We'd have been here in plenty of time if someone hadn't pinched the cab I booked,' said an aggrieved voice beside me.

At the next ticket station stood beanpole man from the spa. The lady beside him was admiring her freshly painted toes, which were decorated with tiny Christmas trees.

The cashier paused, 'I'm really sorry, Sir, the last two seats have just been taken.'

Beanpole man closed his eyes as if in pain and took a deep breath. I turned away quickly, not wanting to be caught staring as I realised that, once again, I was the culprit.

'There are still seats for the action movie?' the cashier suggested, and I couldn't resist looking back and saw him trying to judge if action movies were his grandmother's thing.

'Come on Izzy.'

'They should thank me,' I told Sally as she dragged me away. 'His Gran looked pretty feisty, and he's definitely not the rom-com type.'

Two hours later, Sally and I were ejected from the cosy warmth of the Christmas movie. Inside, snow had been falling, the girl had got her guy, and I felt satisfied that I'd fully celebrated my birthday, and was now ready to greet Christmas.

I had one more job to do, and there was just time before the shops shut.

'Return?' The shop assistant looked scandalised. 'People don't *return* Magic Beads!'

'I'm sure—' I began, but she swept my explanation aside.

'Bead selection is a very personal process.' She conveniently ignored the ready prepared gift packs on the shelves. 'An arrangement for one person is unlikely to match another.'

'But I didn't choose—'

'Besides,' she continued helpfully. 'You don't have the receipt.' She gently nudged me outside and shut the door, propping the 'closed' sign into place.

'You again!' I blinked, still catching my breath. It was beanpole man, and he didn't look pleased to see me. 'You've been one step ahead of me all day, and you've even managed to beat me to the last thing I thought I could get right for my Grandmother.' He gestured to the box.

Something snapped inside me. I'd been trying to get to this rotten shop all day. It was hardly my fault if he hadn't done it either. I pushed the taxi to the back of my mind.

'Here, take the horrid things.' I thrust the box at him and stormed off.

'Hey, wait.' He looked understandably shocked. 'I can't take this!'

'I wish you would,' I said. 'I almost feel I owe it to you.'

'But—! You can't just—!'

'Really,' I said. 'It would make me feel much better.'

His confusion gave way as he saw the determination on my face. 'I'm sorry, I shouldn't have snapped,' he said. 'It was just… seeing the shop shut, and you standing there with the box in your hands, it seemed to represent everything I hadn't achieved all day.'

I laughed. 'You were actually witnessing my utter failure to do the one thing I intended when I got up this morning.'

He held the box out to me. 'Let me buy you a drink, and you can tell me all about it?'

Mum also bought me up to remember 'thank you' notes:

Dear Aunt May,
Thank you for the Magic Beads.
Sometimes gifts can have unexpected benefits, and it's thanks to the beads that I met my new boyfriend, David, that he was able to get his Gran the perfect gift, and, indirectly, that she has developed a passion for getting her toenails painted.

However, maybe next year you could just get me cinema tickets instead, please?

Hope your Christmas was a good as mine!

Love Izzy xx

© Aug 2017

First published as 'The Birthday Girl' in *The People's Friend* Dec 2017

This is a bit of a favourite. I'd been writing a slew of Christmas stories and wanted to put a different spin on it. I wasn't completely sure if The People's Friend would go for it, and was delighted when the fiction editor, Shirley Blair, snapped up my 'mad but fun' story.

JENNY'S LEGACY

'Don't you think it's time we sorted out the house, Molly?'

With those words, Auntie Jenny, who'd always seemed more like a big sister than an auntie, had quietly got us organised. Before we knew it, Sally, Katie and I were in our oldest jeans, equipped with bin liners and boxes to sort through Mum's things.

It was a bit chaotic at first. We didn't really know where to start, and everyone had different priorities.

'Where's Mum's pink scarf?'

'In the charity bag.'

'What!? Why did you put it in there?'

'You always hated it!'

'It's got too many memories to throw it away.'

Gently Auntie Jenny steered us towards the tasks we were best at, Katie collating anything to do with family history, Sally to clear and clean the kitchen and me to go through the books and movies. Then, satisfied that we were all occupied, she left to create one of her smashing picnic lunches.

'Good old Auntie Jenn, she knows an army marches on its stomach!'

'I'm sure she mentioned home baked quiche.'

'Mmm, come on then girls, let's earn it.'

And she was right, of course. We'd been putting this off for ages, but working together made it easier and brought us closer.

By tackling the big, impersonal things first, we soon had bags and boxes marked for various destinations. But I paused on the threshold of Mum's bedroom. 'I think we should do this room together.'

The others joined me, and together it became a trip down memory lane, laughing at some of the hats we found and oohing over her wedding dress, neatly packed away at the back of the wardrobe. Far too small for any of us. Mum, like Auntie Jenny, had been tiny whilst we had all inherited Dad's height.

Going through her dressing table became a team effort rather than the harrowing event it could have been. As oldest, I had her wedding ring, Sally her engagement ring and Katie her gold sovereign.

'Oh look!' Sally held out Mum's farthing ring.

'She loved that ring.' I held out my hand, and Sally reluctantly passed across the old bronze ring set with a tiny coin. 'What sort of bird is it? I never could recall.'

'It's a wren,' said Katie. 'I doubt it's worth anything, but—'

I traced the outline of the bird with its stubby little tail. I wanted this, more than I did Mum's wedding ring. But I could tell that the others did too.

I put it to one side. 'We can decide on that later. Let's tackle another drawer first.'

So we sorted through the odds and ends. Brooches, hairpins, costume jewellery, until tucked right at the back of the drawer I found an old pillbox.

'I don't remember that.'

'Me neither.'

It was small, and rattled. The lid enamelled with two birds in flight.

'Pretty,' I said.

'Go on, open it.'

But there were only coins inside, tarnished with age. The others lost interest, 'Keep it if you like, Molly.' So I put it in my pocket and forgot about it as we carried on.

When we stopped for tea later, I took it out again. There were four pennies inside. One worn, old penny, much larger than the others. Brittania was just recognisable on one side and a young Elizabeth, with a wreath in her hair on the other. The other coins were all new pence.

'That won't get you much,' said Katie as she passed me a mug. 'They aren't even that old, are they?'

I checked the dates. '1971 is the oldest of the new ones. That's when I was born, so you're right, not old at all.'

'Ha ha. What about the other one?'

'No. Even that one's only ten years older.' I dropped them back into the box.

'Wait a minute.' Sally took them out and examined them again. 'Here, look. 1971.' She put that coin next to me. '1974, that's me. And 1976.' She passed the newest coin to Katie.

'Do you think that's it? Pennies for the years we were each born? But what about that one?'

Sally picked up the last coin, squinting to make out the date beneath the tarnish. '1961? She hadn't even met Dad then.'

There was a shocked silence as that sank in, then we all started talking at once.

'No way!'

'Surely not!'

'How old was she then?'

'Nineteen,' said Katie, the family historian. Suddenly she jumped up and dashed from the room.

She was back in no time, carrying the box of photos she'd been sorting through all morning. She dumped them all out on the floor and rummaged through them with utter disregard for the time she'd spent putting them in order.

'What are you doing?' asked Sally.

'Here.' Katie held a photo aloft triumphantly.

'Isn't that Auntie Sheila's wedding? What's so special about that?'

'Auntie Sheila was married in June 1961.'

'I can see that. Look at what Uncle Paul's wearing!'

'And her hair!'

But the plain, high necked, white satin dress, with the full skirt to just below the knee was stunning.

'You're missing the point,' said Katie. 'Look at Gran in the photo.'

Sally and I looked blankly at the photo of Gran, looking smart and trim in a suit. 'What are we supposed to see here?'

Katie shook her head at us. 'Auntie Jenny was born in August 1961.'

We looked again.

'Shouldn't Gran look pregnant then?'

'And where's Mum in this photo?' said Katie pointedly. 'What in the world would make her miss her big sister's wedding?'

'She must be there!' Sally grabbed the picture but couldn't spot Mum anywhere.

'Aren't there any photos of Mum from around that time?' I fanned out the photos on the floor, and the others joined in, but the only pictures of Mum from around that time were headshots.

'That doesn't tell us anything,' said Sally.

'No birth certificates, I suppose?' I looked to Katie.

She shook her head. 'Auntie Jenny would have that.'

'I wonder what it says on it?'

I sorted through the photos on the floor and picked out one of Auntie Jenny. Tiny Auntie Jenny, who looked so much like Mum and had always seemed more like an older sister than an auntie. Auntie Jenny who would be turning up soon with lunch.

As if the thought had triggered the event, we heard the slam of a car door and the click of heels on the path.

'Do you think she knows?'

We stared at each other.

The door opened and we heard bags being placed on the kitchen worktop. The smell of freshly baked quiche drifted through to us.

'How is it going girls? I hope you're hungry!' There was a clatter of crockery.

'What are we going to say?'

I picked up the old penny, so worn from handling, and thought of that other coin with the little Jenny wren on it. Such an appropriate name for that busy little bird. Much as I wanted that ring, I knew it wasn't for me.

I looked up at the others. 'I think we tell her that we know who should have the farthing ring, don't you?'

© July 2016

First published in *The People's Friend* as 'Family Heirlooms' Jan 2017.

My mum had a ring with a farthing set in it. As a child I found it fascinating. When we were going through everything after she died, I kept an eye out for it but never found it. I often wondered what happened to that ring, so I made up a story about it.

I seem to write about rings a lot. I guess they're such a treasure trove of possibilities; memories, promises, dreams…

THE DIRECT APPROACH

'Do I get him something for Christmas, or not?'

My friend, Debbie, had a new man. You'd think that would be a good thing, but although I could hear Slade somewhere, telling us that everybody was having fun, Debbie didn't look so sure.

'Well,' I gazed at the swirl of whipped cream on my hot chocolate. It had arrived as a mouth-watering mountain, topped with chocolate sprinkles, but at this rate, it was going to melt away before I got the chance to demolish it. 'Do you want to buy him something?'

'Of course I do.'

I was about to ask what the problem was, but she cut in first.

'But only if he gets me something.'

'Why wouldn't he?'

'We've only just got together. In fact, it's not even formal yet.'

'Formal?'

'He hasn't actually asked me yet.' She twisted a nut-brown curl around her finger. I envied those curls. Despite years of curling irons, crimpers and one disastrous perm, my hair stayed unapologetically straight. Much like my way of tackling life's problems, whereas Debbie preferred to circle around an issue.

'Asked you what?'

'Out!'

They'd been glued to each other every time I'd seen them. 'How old are you?' I said.

She waved her spoon in the air. How had she managed to finish her cream? 'You don't understand what it's like, Tacy. Christmas is the most awkward time in the world to get together with someone!'

'Oh thanks.' I rescued a dollop of cream before it sank without trace and concentrated on licking the spoon clean, looking anywhere but at Debbie before I throttled her. 'A week ago you were crowing about having someone to smooch on New Year's Eve.' I scooped up another spoonful.

'I'm sorry,' she relented. Then spoiled it by starting again. 'It's just that awkward length of time. If I don't buy him something and he gives me a gift, it'll look mean, but if I do and he doesn't, I'll look too keen.'

By gazing over her shoulder, I'd accidentally been staring right into the hazel eyes of the man at the next table. I flushed as I realised I was still licking the spoon.

I turned back to Debbie. 'Is he getting you anything?'

'I don't know!' she wailed. Jonah Lewie had taken over now and was stopping the cavalry.

I took a deep breath and regretfully stirred the remaining traces of cream into the chocolate. 'Have you tried talking to him?' The man on the next table winked at me, and I realised I was staring over her shoulder again. I dragged my attention back to Debbie.

'I can't do that!' When had my best friend turned into a snivelling mess over a man? And why hadn't I noticed?

Ignoring the rather charming looking man at the next table, I grabbed her phone and tapped in a message before handing it back. 'There,' I said. 'My early Christmas present to you!'

It read: *Dear Gavin, Is there anything in particular you'd like for Christmas? And by the way, Tacy wants to know if she can call you my boyfriend yet? xxx <3 <3 <3*

'Tacy! How could you! Maybe he hasn't got it yet. Can you retrieve texts?' She jabbed buttons frantically.

I couldn't resist checking to see how Charming Man was taking this. He applauded silently.

Suddenly Debbie's phone beeped. 'Oh no, it's Gavin,' she yelped. 'Oh! Oh my! Yes! Thank you, Tacy!' She flung her arms around me, spilling my poor, luke-warm chocolate across the table.

'I take it that's a 'yes' then? Did he say what he wants for Christmas?'

She turned bright red and refused to tell me. Then her phone beeped again.

'Oh, that's Gavin again. D'you mind if I rush off? I'll catch you later, bestest friend.'
With a flurry she was gone, leaving me staring at the ruins of our table.

'Can I get you another drink?' My charming friend from the next table slid into her place and smiled at me again.'I can see that you're a direct sort of girl,' he continued. 'So, what do you want for Christmas?'

Mariah Carey started warbling, *All I want for Christmas.*

© August 2016

First published in *My Weekly* as 'No Time Like the Present' in Dec 2016.

My Weekly changed my main character's name from 'Tacy' to 'Tracey'. Either they thought it was a typo or, more likely, changed it to make it easier for the readers. I actually got the name from Judith Kerr. The little girl in *The Tiger Who Came to Tea* was originally named after her daughter, Tacy, but was changed to 'Sophie' for the same reason.

CLEANERS

God, this was dull. I moved the feather duster lightly over the keyboard, fighting the urge to poke someone with it. Preferably Gordon.

'Don't attract attention with jerky movements. Keep everything smooth.' As his words echoed through my head, it was all I could do to keep smiling. The dry old stick was probably right, but that didn't make me feel any better about being bored out of my skull.

Don't get me wrong, no-one was forcing me to be here. But I'd expected this spy training lark to be more exciting. A bit more kung-fu and sneaking around. Instead, I couldn't help feeling I'd been conned into taking an office cleaning job.

I continued to grumble to myself as I dusted around Mr Oblivious, smiled at Mrs Me-me-me and started cleaning around all the photos on Mr Martyr's desk. The poor guy never sat there; he seemed to spend all his time sorting out everyone else's problems.

Snap out of it Kelly. I gave myself a mental slap as I realised I was in danger of feeling sorry for someone else and knuckled down to my mental exercises.

Dull. But necessary, according to Gordon.

That seat was empty again today. *He* always left his drawers unlocked. *She* hadn't shut down her screen. *That* cupboard was never locked. *That* one usually was.

I glanced around. I didn't usually dust this section; a blind alley of metal storage cabinets guarded by a rottweiler of a blonde with her desk parked across the front.

But Blondie was nowhere in sight today, and the cupboard door, temptingly ajar with its key poking out of the lock was too much for little old me.

I ran my duster across it, removed the key and dropped it into the gap between that cupboard and the next. You never knew what might come in useful another time, but as cleaners were always checked by security you couldn't take anything home. Except your pass, they were provided by the cleaning company.

I turned and nearly ran into the Fat Lady.

'Hello!' she beamed, 'I could do with you at home.'

I laughed dutifully and scarpered. I'd made the mistake of talking to her on my first day, but I'm a fast learner.

'I'm pretty sure she wouldn't want me at home,' I thought, catching a waft of my uniform. Gordon had said it was clean, but I didn't believe him.

The thought of Gordon was like a prod in the back. The mental exercises were crap, but at least they made it less boring.

That meeting room was always full, queue for the drinks machine again, around the corner, hello to the toilet cleaning ladies (thank god I hadn't got *that* job), ho hum, blend, blend, blend…

'You're supposed to blend in,' Gordon had explained two months ago when I'd complained about my oh-so-thrilling cleaning mission. 'It's not all Martinis and roulette tables you know. You're supposed to become invisible.' He'd looked me over with his usual lack of enthusiasm.

So much for the glamorous lifestyle that had been painted for me that first night at the pub. Yeah, that guy had seen me coming alright. Talked me up, made me feel important, then left me with that tantalising card and its solitary phone number.

'Invisible,' I mumbled, 'would probably be easier if I smelled better.'

That evening, as I retrieved my coat and bag from my locker at Clean-eze HQ, I found a post-it note with a message written in smudgy pencil attached to my bag.

Report, was all it said.

Excitement and nerves fluttered in my chest. I tried not to glance around too obviously, wondering how that note had found its way into my supposedly secure locker.

I checked that nothing was missing from my bag, then left.

Gordon's office was in a dreary little building two streets over. You could almost see the tumbleweed drifting across the car park, but the coded entry systems and the spy-eye in the ceiling indicated that someone, somewhere, was watching.

I fought down my usual urge to stick my finger up at it and went in search of my lord and master.

'It's time for a change,' he informed me as I slouched on the desk in front of him.

Finally. But I was damned if I'd let him see my excitement. 'I told you that ages ago.'

'Two months,' he frowned at me. 'Is the perfect length of time for you to become so familiar that people no longer notice you. It also gives you plenty of time to know your surroundings.'

'I really didn't need that long.'

'Tomorrow, when they see you in this, their brains will recognise your face and dismiss the uniform. Nobody will question your presence.'

He laid a suit bag on the table along with a pair of black court shoes. I'd been on my feet in sensible lace-ups all day, and they killed. The thought of being propped up on stilts all day tomorrow made my ankles ache.

Then again, I'd bet the suit smelled better than my cleaning overalls.

'So, what am I meant to do?'

'It's called a fishing trip,' he smirked. 'You take documents from printers, desks, anywhere they won't be easily missed. We then go through them and strip out all sorts of useful information.'

'It seems a bit random to me. Can't you just pinpoint if there's anything specific you're after?' I suggested. 'You know, sneak into the boardroom in the dead of night and open the safe with a stethoscope.'

'Special missions are for those who have been through advanced training.' God, the man had no sense of humour. 'This is bread and butter work, suitable as a training mission while you're still expendable.'

Well, screw you Gordon, I'll show you. Expendable indeed.

'Don't get any ideas,' he added. 'Any foul-ups and we'll drop you like a hot potato.'

The next morning, suited up and with my cleaner's pass giving me access, I merged with the throng of employees clicking their way through the entrance doors of Axiom Systems. *Bring it on.*

I'd planned what to do over and over, and as everyone streamed off to their boring little jobs, I took cover in the loos while they settled in.

I picked a floor and headed down the office to the printer. I took everything from the tray and pretended to flick through it as I walked back. *Easy peasy, no eye contact. Look away please everyone, nothing to see here.*

'Hey, excuse me.'

They aren't talking to me, carry on.

'Excuse me, Miss?' A hand caught my arm.

Ohmygod, busted already! What had I done wrong?

I turned. It was Mr Martyr, holding a piece of paper.

Bloody man. Couldn't he mind his own business for once?

'You dropped this.'

I managed a kind of choked gurgle, 'Thank you.'

'First day? You'll be fine.' He smiled at me and walked away.

I looked at the paper I was holding, now crumpled and a bit damp with perspiration. I hoped he was right.

I ducked into the nearest toilet and examined the rings of sweat that had appeared under my armpits. All that from one confrontation? Jeez. Was that why

Gordon had included the jacket? I couldn't imagine him ever building up a sweat.

I had to push myself to go back out there. My run-in with Mr Martyr had shaken me more than I'd realised.

Gradually I fell into a rhythm, affecting a preoccupied air as I moved from office to office, printer to printer. When I had a large enough pile of paper, I'd grab an envelope from the nearest stationery cupboard, write down the PO box number that Gordon had made me memorise and slip it into the nearest post tray.

A couple of times I pretended to leave notes on desks, dropping my paper on top of a likely looking stack and sweeping the lot up as I left.

'Hello, when did you start working here?'

Oh great. Of all the people to recognise me, it had to be the Fat Lady.

'You're a fast mover, I swear it was only yesterday I saw you with a feather duster in your hand.'

It was only yesterday. I needed to say something quickly before she actually tried thinking.

'Ah well, that's agency work for you. Cinderella one day, office junior the next.' I moved to head off, but my usual duck and weave didn't work today.

'Which agency? We're always on the lookout for good people.'

'Uh, it uses a couple of different names.' Somehow I didn't think Gordon would thank me for blurting them out though.

'That's ok, I can look them up.' Meeting her eyes, like little black currants in that big doughy face, I realised she wasn't as dumb as I'd thought and a bead of sweat trickled down my neck.

'I… uh…' as I shifted the paperwork in my arms I saw her foot twitch impatiently and, failing any better idea, I faked a fumble sending papers fluttering to the floor.

'Oh sh…' I dropped to my knees, scooping them back up as quickly as I could and used the diversion to change the subject. 'Look, I'd love to catch up, but I've got to get these to my boss…'

Shaking my head in apology, I dashed off not daring to look back to where she must be staring suspiciously after me.

I took refuge in another toilet cubicle, burying my face against my knees.

Idiot. Why hadn't I prepared for anything like that? Come to think of it, why hadn't Gordon?

As I stared at the grout between the floor tiles, I realised there was a lot that Gordon hadn't prepared me for. Was that a test or did he want me to fail?

I plucked at my blouse, clammy with sweat. How much longer did I need to stay? I couldn't picture myself queueing in the canteen with these people, but I was damned if I'd give Gordon any reason to be smug by leaving too soon.

I scuttled out and headed straight upstairs. Gaining a new floor helped me feel a bit calmer and I returned to grabbing and posting, but my confidence had been sucked away by the Fat Lady's currant bun eyes.

I passed the cupboard that had been unlocked the day before and noticed that it had been locked again. Peering down the gap I could see that the key was still where I'd dropped it. What could be so important that someone had found a replacement key?

I stuck my pen in the gap and tried to draw it towards me, but it was just out of reach. Casting around, I found a paper clip and wound it around the end of the pen, creating a hook. That was better.

Eventually, I dragged the key out and turned it triumphantly in the lock.

'Oh great.' A row of champagne bottles, two calculators and a projector.

Disgusted, I started to close the door, but noticed something tucked on the top shelf. There was a small pile of documents with something official-looking on the front. With my luck it was probably the office seating plan, but as I crouched there debating its worth I heard footsteps and swiped the lot in a moment of panic.

Blondie-the-Rottweiler's laugh drifted towards me as I fumbled with the lock, and I realised that the only escape route was past her.

'Thank god I had a spare, I'd have been fried.' Was she talking about the key?

Crap. Come on Kelly, don't get caught on your hands and knees. Think girl.

'No, nothing missing.' The click of heels came closer.

Yes, definitely talking about the key. No way did I want to get caught loitering here. There must be somewhere to hide.

'I printed that report for you earlier...'

Under the desk? Not a chance. Behind the plant? *Yeah, right dummy.*

'I'll just get it for you.'

Her voice was practically in my ear; she must be just around the corner.

Come on, come on. Think of something.

'No, it's no trouble...'

Oh God. I crammed myself into the bottom shelf of a metal filing rack and tried to pull the roller cover down. I had to hook a finger around the bottom to stop it from pinging back up.

A blind person couldn't fail to notice me.

Blondie came round the corner and rummaged on the desk.

'Oh hang on, this is the March report...'

There was the squeak of a drawer opening. Sweat dripped off my nose. This must be the only cupboard that hadn't been dusted in years.

'Didn't you need April's? Let me just...' More rustling.

Why hadn't I just stood up and walked past them? Duh! What an idiot!

A chair creaked and I heard keys tapping.

The dust was making my nose itch. *Piss off Blondie.* I felt a sneeze building.

'There you go. I'll just print that off. Let's go wait at the printer. Nothing seems to be coming through today; I swear it's that girl from Legal...'

I rolled out of the cupboard, making a half-hearted attempt to brush off the dust as her footsteps faded up the hall. God only knew what my hair looked like.

I disposed of my haul into the post and decided to call it a day. If Gordon didn't like it, he could blow it out his old wazoo. I'd had enough.

A week later, I found an envelope stuffed through my letterbox.

I hadn't heard a word from Gordon and was sure I'd screwed up somehow. Part of me, still shaky from my near miss, wanted to leave things there and pretend it had never happened. I dumped the local paper I'd bought for the jobs section on the kitchen table and ripped open the envelope.

Neatly bound stacks of money tumbled out.

I gave a shaky laugh as I flicked through one of the bundles to prove it was real. What the hell had I done to earn this much? Had they made a mistake?

Glancing down, trying to calculate how much was there, I caught a headline I'd missed earlier.

Fired father of four denies stealing confidential documents.

Mr Martyr stared back at me from the page.

Nonono. Coincidence, that was all. Even as I tried not to look, other words, *Axiom... 29th May*, jumped out at me.

There had to be a mistake. I picked up the envelope and something else slid out.

It looked like a still shot from a security camera. Me in that damned suit turning the lock on that bloody cupboard. The *Axiom Systems* banner was clear on the wall behind me and the digital imprint of the date in the bottom corner read *29th May*.

Stuck on the front was a post-it note with a message in faint smudgy pencil. *Report for next assignment. Tuesday 7.30pm.*

© 2011

This is from my early writing days when I thought I was going to write thrillers. Inspired by years of working in an office, when day after day I'd watch the cleaners pass by often having to dust ridiculous things like notice-boards. I concluded that they would probably make pretty good double agents.

NINE LADIES DANCING

'You're going to have to do it without me,' Liza had said on the phone this morning. 'I've come down with some sort of bug. It must have been something I ate.'

That was why I, Katie Parrish, sensible mum of three and member of the PTA, was about to do the most embarrassing thing I'd ever done, in the middle of a shopping centre on a December Saturday.

It was all Liza's fault. Friend and dance teacher, she'd come up with the idea of a flashmob to drum up new members for her Salsa classes.

'What's a flashmob?' I'd asked cautiously.

'You see them on the internet all the time,' she'd replied. 'When people suddenly start dancing in the middle of the street. It's great fun and looks spur of the moment.'

The doubt must have shown on my face, because she shrugged and said, 'The other idea I had was one of those calendars. You know, where we're all tastefully nude and strategically covered—'

'We'll do the flashmob thing,' I said.

'You'll get to wear a sparkly dress,' she promised.

I'd always had a weak spot for the chance to glam up.

But Liza was supposed to be the leader. She was meant to be the one who started dancing alone in the middle of the arcade, right where nobody could miss her.

Liza. Not me.

'Go on Katie, you can do it!' Pam shoved me forward before I could think too much, and I stumbled to the spot where, when the music started, I'd drop my coat to reveal the thankfully-not-too-skimpy dance outfit, complete with promised spangles.

As the first notes of Latin music spilled out of the sound system, I caught sight of my fifteen-year-old son, Ash, with a group of friends. As if things couldn't get any worse.

But it was too late to warn him. I threw my head back and dropped my coat, counting the beat before taking my first steps.

Liza was meant to have done this first part, then gradually the rest of us, disguised as Christmas shoppers, would in turn ditch their coats and bags to join in. As I spun and waggled my fingers to encourage Liz and Maggie to join me, I saw the back of Ash's head as he slunk into a sports shop. Was it better or worse that he was pretending not to know me?

We had to adjust our spacing to allow for Liza's absence, and concentrating on the steps helped me ignore the crowd. One, two, three, *pause*. Five, six, seven, *pause*. Left hand turn, cha cha cha, then back to the right. People began to clap in time, and I couldn't help grinning when I heard a *Whoop!* from somewhere.

'Sorry to embarrass you in front of your mates, Ash,' I thought. 'I promise that this won't ever happen again.'

There was another solo coming up, but I didn't feel so alone this time as the others were with me. Behind me, Pam and Liz rhumba'd from side to side, while Frankie and Gentian, our youngest members, did the same in front. To my left and right, Maggie, Claire, Linzi and Danielle salsa'd back and forth. Meanwhile, in the centre, I tried to remember the moves I'd only practised a few times before today.

'Don't worry so,' Liza had said. 'You can do it. And even if you do fluff one of the steps, I doubt anyone in the audience will know. Just *look* confident.'

But I'd know. Liza would know. Pam would know, because that was the sort of thing she looked out for. And, knowing my luck, Craig Revel Horwood would happen past too. Thank goodness Ash, at least, had been kind enough to stay away.

The tempo increased and I had to concentrate on the twists and turns, hips swaying and arms circling to the rhythm of the Cuban beat. And then I had a brainwave.

My dress. My beautiful magenta, sparkly dress, gathered at the left knee to show off my footwork. But at the back was a sweeping train that I could swish about for effect.   Maybe, just maybe if I swished in the right direction, it would cover up any faults.

But then I took my final turn, and I was so horrified by what I saw that I completely forgot to worry about my steps.

As we finished with a flourish and a clap, striking a pose, I realised that we were lined up directly opposite Ash and his friends outside the sports shop.

The music stopped, and I swear my heart did too.

But then with a fantastic display of timing, they each drew a table tennis bat from behind their backs, with a hastily scrawled '10' on each one.

© Aug 2017

First published in *My Weekly* Dec 2017

This was my first commission by a national magazine (ok, and my only one so far!)

The fiction editor at My Weekly had the brainwave for a fiction Christmas special with a story for each line of 'The Twelve Days of Christmas'.

I was able to draw on my own flashmob experience from when my friend, Pam, talked me into taking part in one in the middle of Exeter. It was great fun and we must have been pretty good as our local John Lewis asked us to repeat it in their store a couple of months later!

SLEEPING BEAUTY

'I passed the postman in the lane.' Fiona held out a letter. 'Funny to see your full name, you've been 'Busy Bea' for as long as I can remember.'

She was right. The nickname had been a part of me for so long that I'd named my garden restoration firm after it. No one called me Beatrix except Jake, and that scrawl of black ink on the envelope was unmistakably his hand.

Trust him to take the old fashioned route of pen to paper. Always determined to leave his mark on the world rather than trust anything as ephemeral as email.

There had been a time I'd found the notes he left for me romantic. Not for a while though, and I certainly didn't need an audience for whatever he might have to say now.

'Thanks.' I shoved it in my pocket.

'Nothing important then?'

'Nothing that can't wait.'

'Ok. So what did you want to show me then?'

As usual, I couldn't tell if Fiona was being tactful or oblivious, but I was grateful for the change of subject.

'Over here.' I steered her past the rubbish pile before she could ruin her heels and guided her to the old rose garden I'd been excavating.

When Fiona, an old schoolfriend, had contacted me to renovate the garden of her latest investment, I'd wondered if she saw me as a project too. I'd been determined to show that my skills made such thoughts unnecessary, but had failed miserably when my life imploded a month ago.

Without batting an eyelid, she'd offered me the cottage to stay in. It was, as she said, close to work and the lack of rent was balanced by my having to shift rooms now and then to accommodate the builders.

'This place is a dream to work on. As I get through the worst, I'm starting to see the shape it once was. Look,' I led her along a pathway where the overgrown rose bushes had created a leafy tunnel, and pointed out the beautifully detailed nameplates I'd started to uncover for each plant. 'Someone really loved this garden once.'

'Sleeping Beauty.' She ran a nail along one as she read it and then tilted her head. It had rained earlier and the afternoon sun was working on the damp petals and soil to bring out a heady mix of scents. 'Oh my, that's gorgeous. Although,' she eyed the branches above us doubtfully, 'do you intend to leave them like this?'

'No. I'm just being cautious at the moment. Getting a feel for the shape that exists underneath all this rather than running the risk of losing something special by hacking it all back.'

'What's this?' She hooked something out of the branches that I, at my smaller height, had missed.

'Another one. I keep finding these.' I turned the wooden apple in her hand to show a heart shaped slice across the front with an ornately carved 'M' inside it. 'I wondered at first if they were markers of some kind, but the letters don't match the plants.'

'Reminds me of the treasure hunts we had as kids.' She traced the letter, weighing the apple in her hand.

'Wasn't the old guy who used to live here a carpenter? Maybe he made them.' I shrugged, keen to move on and show her my find from this morning.

'Mmm, could be. It looks pretty old and this place hasn't been touched in years.'

'I can believe that.' I mentally reviewed the latest scratches on my arms and considered her linen suit. Perhaps dragging her through the ruins of this garden hadn't been such a good idea.

'Were these what you wanted to show me?'

'No, here.' I led her further along to the grotto I'd unearthed. 'I came across it this morning. With the rain dripping through the leaves it felt like the saddest place in the world.'

'You worked this morning? But it was raining.'

I laughed. 'In this job you can't let the weather scare you off.'

She looked slightly horrified and looked away to hide it, taking in the scene before her. 'What a mess. Do you think it was vandalised?'

'I don't know. I don't think so because this is the only place to show this kind of damage.' I knelt and tried to stand Eros, or whoever it was supposed to be, in position but he was in too many pieces to be up to the job. Once Fiona had got the idea of him, hands cupped beside the small waterfall that trickled into a tiny pool ringed with frolicking nymphs, I replaced him. 'Someone really took it out on poor old Eros,' I said.

'Oh!' I turned at her indrawn breath. 'I remember now. The estate agent had some tale about the old man who lived here. About how years ago he'd quarrelled with his sweetheart but then she died in a car crash before they could patch things up. I dismissed it at the time as a story for the sale and to excuse why the garden was so overgrown.'

'Why would a car crash have anything to do with the garden?'

'Something about how he'd created the rose garden for her and wouldn't let anyone touch it afterwards.'

'But that's awful,' I objected. 'The sitting room looks straight out on this. If that were true, he'd spend every day of his life watching it get worse.'

'Quite,' she agreed, missing the point. Although to be honest I wasn't completely sure what point I was trying to make. She tapped the wooden apple, 'Let me know if you find any more of these, they're rather cute. Maybe we can find a use for them.'

After she'd left, I returned to the grotto, trying to put together the ghost of its former glory and determine if it were worth saving.

But left to myself I couldn't ignore the crackle of paper in my back pocket. I pulled out Jake's letter.

Dear Beatrix,

I've given you time and space to think, but surely a month is enough? You knew I might have to work. I explained that, and you were ok about it. If there was a problem you should have said something; we're a team aren't we? The girl I fell in love with knew the importance of following our dreams and that we could work out anything else.

I'm here until the fifteenth. If I don't hear from you by then, I guess I was wrong about that girl.

I hope not.

Jake.

'Hardly the romantic apology I was hoping for,' I snorted.

Then I realised that, stupidly, that was what I'd been hoping for, even though deep down I'd known it would never be Jake's style.

Furious with myself, I looked around for something to throw, but the grotto was in pretty bad shape already. I started tearing up weeds instead.

Of *course* I'd changed. Yes, I was still that girl who wanted to follow her dreams. But those dreams were different now.

There was a time I'd shared his thrill of flitting off to exciting places, discovering exotic plants while he took photos. But over the last year or so my gardening business had kept me grounded, and just like my plants, I found I wanted to put down roots. But Jake hadn't seemed bothered if I went with him or not.

I sniffed hard and refused to cry. Holding on to the anger I'd been keeping close ever since my birthday, a month ago.

The night I'd gritted my teeth through the agony of pretending to all our friends that it was fine, just fine that he couldn't make it to my party. That dressing up and seeing everyone was fun enough. What, after all, was a thirtieth compared to a photoshoot in Paris?.

And it was partly my fault. I'd made the noises that it wasn't a big deal, but of course it was a big deal. He was supposed to get the hint. But he never did, I always seemed to have to spell these things out to him.

Yeah, that old story. I know. And please don't see me as the put upon little woman because I love my job. Really, give me some seeds and some soil to plant them in and I'm happy as a pig in mud.

Who needs Paris?

I tried to concentrate on putting Eros back together. His hands were too caked in dirt to balance on his outstretched arms so I started to wipe it away, attempting to prise out the lump between his cupped palms.

But it was stuck fast and, as I rinsed it in the murky coffee grounds of the pool I found another of those funny little apples. This one rotten, with a barely recognisable 'E' to go with the 'M' we'd found earlier.

'ME,' I said aloud. Then stopped as I remembered Fiona's comment about treasure hunts, and ran to fetch the other apples.

I sat cross-legged next to Eros as I laid them out before me, M, E, R, R, Y, A, M, switching them around a few times until I was happy with the results.

I sank back on my heels imagining how the grotto must have once looked, with sunshine dappling through the leaves, the heady aromatic spell of the roses and the steady trickle of the waterfall where Eros knelt, hands outstretched with his promise of love.

I knew only too well how it felt to have somebody spoil a moment you'd been anticipating for ages.

I picked up Eros's hands again, and this time the lump came away easily. It was a box.
I think I knew then, but I still felt a shock of awe as I eased it open and saw the ring inside. The gold was undimmed by the years and the afternoon sun picked out an answering gleam in the diamond.

What had their argument been about, I wondered as I looked again at the row of carved apples.

Marry me, they spelled.

'I'm such an idiot.' I pulled out Jake's letter, smoothing the crumpled paper as the words jumped out at me.

We're a team… We could work out anything…

I didn't need Paris or a fancy birthday party, but perhaps I did need a mind reader. Failing that, maybe I should actually try *talking* to Jake. Like we used to.

I thought of that old man, sitting silently through the years watching the weeds and brambles cloak his monument to his dead love, like Sleeping Beauty's palace, with only the bitter ashes of his anger for company.

How many times must he have wished he could turn the clock back, to take back the angry words and rush after her before it was too late?

'Not me,' I said and ran to grab my car keys.

© Nov 2011

First published in *The People's Friend* as 'Different Dreams' June 2016.

This was the first story I ever sold to a national magazine. It went through a lot of different versions and sat on my hard drive for a long time while I tried to work out what to do with it.

It was only when I took it to my writing group for critique that the wonderful Margaret James said, 'Do you want to write for the women's magazines, because this is exactly what they're looking for.' Without those words I'd never have dreamed of sending it to *The People's Friend*. Luckily for me, they accepted it and the rest, as they say, is history.

(The moral of that tale? Don't let your story sit on a shelf. Get someone to look at it; send it off. Even if it gets rejected, at least you've done something with it!)

PROJECT: ROMANCE

'Jim and Dan, Could you hang back for a few minutes?'

Jim held back a sigh as Bryan closed the office door behind the rest of the team. Bryan had been looking more and more highly strung lately.

Dan checked his watch, 'I've got another meeting in ten minutes, Bryan. Will this take long?'

'No, no.' Bryan fidgeted as he resumed his seat, aligning his pen neatly with his notepad. Finally he looked up, 'I've got a secret project to propose to you.'

Jim straightened. This sounded more like it; he was ready for something new.

'It's not work-related,' Bryan said quickly. 'It's just that... well, I had an idea. And as we're all in similar circumstances, I thought we could support each other.'

'What do you mean by 'similar circumstances'?' asked Jim. Bryan was twelve years older than him and two grades higher. Jim played football every Wednesday and attended a local boardgames cafe once a week, while Bryan had two children and a DIY hobby. As for Dan, his children had flown the nest, and he seemed to be on an endless hunt for a hobby to fill the gap.

'We all have wives to keep happy,' Bryan explained.

Dan looked up indignantly, 'I think you'll find that Julie is perfectly satisfied.'

'It's been bothering me ever since Scott and Debbie split up,' Bryan continued as if Dan hadn't spoken. 'We think we're getting along fine, doing what we're supposed to, when suddenly, Bam! You don't surprise her anymore; the magic has gone and she needs to 'find herself'.' He mimicked quotation marks with his index fingers.

'I thought Debbie found herself with Colin from Marketing,' murmured Dan.

'Well, she shouldn't have had to!' Bryan slammed his hand down on the desk. 'And it's not going to happen to us. Oh no! We,' he jabbed his index finger at them, 'are not going to be caught napping. That's why I'm launching 'Project Romance'.'

Jim opened his mouth to say that his wife, Linzi wouldn't be seen dead with Colin from Marketing, but snapped it shut as he recalled that she did karate while he played football and had commented a few times on how 'buff' the instructor was.

'Tell me more about Project Romance,' he said instead.

'Good man.' Bryan snapped his fingers at him. 'We look at certain dates on the calendar. For instance, Valentine's day is coming up—'

'That's ages away,' objected Dan.

'It's four weeks,' Bryan corrected him. 'How many times has it crept up on you unawares? Romance comes naturally to women, but we need to treat it like a project. We put it in the diary, then we work out our objectives and we plan for it. This is war, chaps, and we are not going to get shot down in our prime like Scott was!'

Jim looked over at Dan and shrugged. He was fairly sure that he and Linzi were ok, but where was the harm in planning for Valentine's?

Jim checked himself out in the mirror and undid his top button again. Bryan wouldn't approve, but Linzi had bought him the orange shirt for Christmas, whereas if he got dressed up in some kind of penguin suit, she'd be too busy laughing at him to notice any romance.

The doorbell rang, and he heard Linzi answer it. He checked the tickets in his back pocket for the fifth time and hoped whoever it was didn't plan on staying for long.

'Sure, come on in,' he heard Linzi say. 'Jim,' she called. 'It's Gemma.'

'Who?' The only Gemma he knew was… '*Bryan's* Gemma?'

'I hope you don't mind,' Gemma hovered just inside the door.

'Of course not. Come in and have a cup of tea.' Linzi, clad in jeans and a 'winter is coming' T-shirt, swept her through to the kitchen, smiling approval at his shirt on her way past. That was the trouble with surprises. How was he supposed to get her to dress up if she didn't know what to expect? Did she even realise what day it was? He followed them into the kitchen, getting out mugs as Linzi filled the kettle.

'It's Bryan,' said Gemma as she perched on a chair. 'I'm worried about him.'

Jim was worried about him too. Bryan would be at home right now ready to launch the results of Project Romance at Gemma like a party popper. But she was here! If Bryan found out that he was involved in a delay to his evening's plans there'd be hell to pay. And Jim had his own timescales to meet too.

'He seems so... uptight these days. He's so highly strung that I'm terrified he's going to have some kind of breakdown, but he won't *talk* to me.' She looked over at Jim. 'I wondered if anything was going on at work?'

He gaped at her as all their Project Romance plans flashed through his mind. 'You know Bryan, he likes to give a hundred and ten per cent, but there's nothing you need to worry about.' He resolutely did *not* look at the clock as it ticked towards seven o'clock. Then inspiration struck, and he smiled at her, 'D'you know what I think he really needs?'

She shook her head helplessly.

'He needs to relax and spend Valentine's evening with his wife.'

'I doubt if Bryan even realises what day it is,' she gratefully took the mug Linzi held out.

'Oh, you might be surprised.' He took the mug from her and clasped her hands in his. 'You're right, he has been a bit tense lately. But I think all he really needs is to be reminded of the love and support he has at home with you.' He guided her gently back towards the front door.

'You're sure?'

'I'm very sure.' He held out her coat.

'Why did I never notice what a smooth talker you are?' said Linzi as he closed the door.

'Probably because I've never needed to smooth talk you.'

She grinned, 'I'll take that as a compliment.'

'Good, because it's supposed to be one.' He gazed down at her, not caring what she was wearing, just glad that she didn't feel the need to talk to his work colleagues. He pulled the tickets out of his pocket and presented them to her, 'Speaking of Valentine's, I wondered if you'd like to join me this evening?'

She studied the tickets and bit her lip. His stomach dropped as she looked up at him. 'Actually,' she said. 'If you don't mind, I'd rather not.'

Next morning, Jim was relieved to discover that Gemma had kept her visit to herself. Bryan was going to be upset enough once he learned of last night's unexpected events. Jim had hoped to lurk at the back of the office during their tea break, but Dan insisted on propping the wall up, claiming a back injury.

'So, how did we all do last night?' Bryan peered around expectantly.

Jim blew on the surface of his tea and adjusted the wayward tilt of the swivel chair.

'Come on,' Bryan encouraged. 'Time to report on Project Romance. Who's going first?'

Jim swivelled hopefully in Dan's direction. Bryan had put so much effort into this project and Jim was dreading having to reveal how much he'd failed.

'Ok, I'll start shall I?' said Bryan when the silence had stretched on for too long. 'I really did my homework and read a couple of those romances, e-book versions of course so that no-one would know. I put red roses all round the house, lit a few candles and scattered rose petals in the bath.'

'You really went to town.' Dan had braced his back against the wall and seemed to be pretending to sit on an invisible chair.

'I told you, there's no point in half measures. We have to mean business. Are you feeling alright, Dan?'

'Yes, I'm fine.' Dan straightened up quickly, wincing as something went into spasm. 'Carry on, Bryan.'

'I had a table for two booked at Pablo's, and I spent the evening talking like Elvis, using some of the lines I got from the books.'

'Well done,' said Jim. 'Did Gemma like it?'

'I hope so.' Bryan ran a finger along the inside of his shirt collar and Jim caught sight of a red mark, as if his tux had been too tight. 'How about you, Dan?'

'Well, I did some research too.' Dan checked that the door was shut. 'I read *that* book. You know, the saucy one with the cable ties. I wish I'd thought of using an e-reader. I had some near misses getting caught with it.'

'What book?' Bryan looked confused.

'You know, everyone was reading it last year.' Jim nearly overbalanced his chair as he swung back to Dan. 'What did you do?'

Dan hesitated. 'I don't think you need to know the details. Needless to say, Julie seemed to enjoy herself.'

'If you come up with a successful strategy, you should share it with the rest of the team.' Bryan sounded annoyed.

Dan's cheeks were flushed. 'I really don't think you want to know, Bryan.'

'Have you got some kind of injury, Dan?' Jim tried to change the subject.

'Hmm. You might say that Julie was a bit too enthusiastic.'

'Will somebody *please* explain—?' Bryan looked back and forth at them, frustrated by this verbal game of piggy-in-the-middle.

'I'll lend you the book, Bryan. How did you do, Jim?' Dan turned carefully to him.

Jim looked down into his cup; he knew Bryan wasn't going to like this. 'I'm really sorry guys, I failed. I was all set to take Linzi to a romantic movie, when she presented me with tickets to watch the original Star Wars trilogy back-to-back. She said that Valentine's is for men too.'

Bryan shook his head. 'You're missing the point, Jim. We're not doing this for fun. It's an attempt to set a support network in place in the event of a failure. You don't want to end up like Scott and Debbie, do you?'

'You're letting the side down,' chimed in Dan. 'Man-up, and stick to your guns next time.'

'But I honestly don't think she wanted to see '*Love truly, madly, sleeplessly*'.'

'Of course she did, she's a woman.'

'He's right Jim. You must try harder next time.'

Dan blinked, 'Next time?'

It dawned on Jim suddenly that Bryan was wrong. He hadn't failed, because his and Linzi's relationship didn't *need* fixing. When he'd cautiously mentioned her karate instructor last night, she'd nearly choked on her gin and tonic. Then she'd dryly informed him that as her instructor hadn't a hope of being on the winning team with her at the games cafe, she'd stick with Jim.

'Bryan,' he said. 'When you were talking like Elvis last night, did you listen to what Gemma said back to you?'

'What do you mean?'

Jim took a deep breath. 'I mean that Dan looks as if he might not survive a 'next time', and Linzi and I enjoyed Star Wars so much last night that we've booked to go to a science fiction convention in New York over Easter.'

For once, Bryan was at a loss for words, and Jim smiled at him. 'Maybe Scott and Debbie's relationship was broken, but that doesn't mean that yours is. It's not a war, Bryan. But you're right that it's a project, and Gemma isn't some ornament to be dusted off and admired occasionally, she's your partner. What she thinks is a lot more important than what you *think* she thinks.'

They left Bryan in his office, looking thoughtful. Dan paused outside, 'I don't think Bryan's ready for that book, do you?'

Jim copied the look that Linzi had given him in the pub last night, 'Don't lend Bryan the book, Dan. Just imagine what projects he might dream up!'

Originally titled 'The Let's Keep Our First Wives Club', this started life as another homework piece for my writing group. We had a prompt of 'Valentines' but everything I tried just seemed trite until I decided to turn it on its head and use the men's points of view. Every now and then I start to adjust it to meet the criteria of a magazine story until I realise that I've missed the boat for Valentine's submissions and put it aside for another year. So instead I shall set it free here and it can stop nagging me from my hard-drive.

STAYING ON TRACK

The quiet carriage, with its view of the driver leaning casually against the controls, didn't have the crowd Peter needed to lose himself in.

But there was less chance of a knife in the ribs.

He concentrated on looking inconspicuous, acutely conscious of the papers taped to his chest, crumpled and clammy now after his flight. He could only pray the ink hadn't run.

He looked back at the driver, and a chill shuddered down his spine as he took in the unnatural angle of his head. With no driver to negotiate the complicated track system it was only a matter of time before the train derailed.

Tension thrummed through his body and a bead of sweat trickled down his face. The poor bastard next to him must be near dead from exhaustion not to notice, but that was what years of fear and repression under Hitler had done. These people had shut themselves off from the horror around them, but it wouldn't stop them from denouncing him to save their own skin.

That was what he and others like him were fighting so hard to stop, why the papers plastered to his skin were so desperately important and why *nothing* must prevent him from completing this mission.

It was also why he couldn't sit by and watch all these people die without lifting a finger to help.

As he moved, his neighbour's hand shot out and clamped around his arm, pinning him back into his seat.

Icy blue eyes glared into his. 'Do not move.' The man hissed.

Peter strained against him. 'You don't understand.'

'Yes. I do.'

The man shifted his arm to display the design on his inner wrist.

The Unbroken Circle. Suicide vigilantes, they only received the tattoo when assigned to a mission they wouldn't return from.

The man nodded. 'The guards in the next carriage *must not* reach their destination.'

'Kill them then.' Peter gritted his teeth. 'You don't have to involve the rest of us.'

'It must look like an accident.'

'Look,' he tried. 'We're on the same side. I'm on an important mission.'

'As are we all, my friend. You will stay here with me.' The arm clamped back across him.

'Bloody fanatics.' As he threw himself against the other man, the door at the far end of the carriage snapped open.

Hope flared briefly in his chest, then fizzled out and died.

It was the Sector Commandant, flanked by two officers.

They were looking for him.

Blue-eyes shouted and launched himself down the carriage, as did several others who had been seated quietly.

Peter took advantage of the furore.

It didn't last long. The guards from the next carriage soon overpowered the dissidents.

'Driver,' ordered the Commandant. 'Stop at the next station to dispose of these prisoners.'

Peter turned and saluted, bringing his fingers to the brim of the driver's hat, then leaned casually back against the controls.

© 2013

First published in the 2014 National Flash Fiction Day 'Flashflood'.

Years back I took Holly Lisle's free three-week flash fiction course, *How to write flash fiction that doesn't suck.* If you're looking for an on-line writing community with great courses, Holly's Writing School is a great choice. *Staying on Track* came out of this course, and Holly' advice on structure is something that I still use now in short stories as well as flash fiction.

THE PERFECT CHRISTMAS

'This is my first Christmas in my own place,' I told my flatmate, Rachel. 'I want to do everything properly.'

Rachel didn't look so sure. 'A traditional Christmas isn't all it's cracked up to be, Tilly.'

'That's because you've been brought up on traditional festivities,' I said. 'My family is obsessed with bargains.'

'What's wrong with a bargain?'

'Nothing,' I replied. 'Except when it's taken to extremes. I've never had a Christmas that wasn't cut-rate. The one year we had a real tree, the needles had fallen out by Christmas Eve. The rest of the time we had a fake one that was too tall.'

'Surely that's not so bad?'

'It bent sideways across the ceiling. We had the only star I've ever seen that you had to duck to avoid.'

I saw Rachel trying not to laugh.

'We never had stockings,' I continued. 'We used pillowcases instead.'

'Very practical,' she approved. 'Much easier to fit presents into.'

'No magic,' I retorted.

'Is it magic you want, or tradition?' she said. 'They aren't always the same thing. I love your family's Christmases.'

'That's because they're a novelty to you. This year I want Christmas puddings made with love and a sixpence inside. I want mulled wine and carols on Christmas Eve. And every gift is going to be personal, not dictated by how many you get for free.'

It could have been the noise from passing traffic, but it sounded as if Rachel muttered, 'Good luck with that,' as she turned away.

Although we'd been friends for years, she'd never understood my envy of how normal her family was. But this year I didn't need to be. It was going to be the best Christmas ever.

It wasn't easy being perfect, but it was fun trying. I planned it all out on a spreadsheet, which I printed out and pinned to the kitchen wall, using different coloured highlighters to show my progress.

Hand-making cards was sticky, but fun, and the results definitely had a certain charm to them.

Making my own wrapping paper was a challenge until, flicking through a craft book that I'd got for my niece, I found the perfect solution. And once I'd finished, it seemed a shame not to wrap up the stamping kit I'd used as an extra gift for her.

I bought one of those machines at the posh cook shop that chewed up everything you fed into it and churned it out as mincemeat at the other end. That was quite messy too, and I dented the kitchen table where you had to clamp the machine to it. The results looked good in a fancy jar, though.

On the other hand, I was a complete failure at pastry. Three times I tried, and each time it turned out as a grey, crumbly mess. In the end, I gave in and cheated when I found that you could buy it ready-made, in the chilled aisle at the supermarket. I was sure that Rachel wouldn't mind, and I even got the brand that wasn't on buy-one-get-one-free to make myself feel better.

Rachel put up with all this, even though I could tell she thought I was crazy.

'Have you seen my box of Christmas cards?' she asked one day, as I was faithfully feeding brandy to my homemade cake. 'I left them on the top shelf of the cupboard so I wouldn't disturb the *Feng Shui* of your perfect Christmas.'

I gulped and accidentally slopped in more brandy than I should have.

The trouble with having friends for years is that they don't miss a thing. 'What have you done?' she said.

'I found them yesterday and thought I must have bought them in the January sales.'

'Ye-es…?'

I cringed a bit before I continued, 'So, to make myself feel better about it, I got out the pinking shears and cut them up for gift tags.'

Rachel was silent for so long that I started to *really* worry. After all, her family did this so well, they probably spent a fortune on personalised cards. Just how much had my mistake cost her?

'I'll... I'll hand-make some for you to make up for it,' I offered.

'No,' she sounded stifled, and if it weren't for how serious it was, I'd have thought she was laughing. 'That's not necessary.'

She took it very well, and she must have got replacements from somewhere, maybe some special website for family cards. I walked on eggshells for the next couple of weeks up to Christmas as I didn't want to upset her. The funny thing was, she seemed to be doing the same.

Finally, on Christmas Eve, I was ready to purchase THE TREE.

'Of course I'll come,' said Rachel when I asked if she'd like to come with me. 'It'll be my tree too, you know. We'll go halfsies.'

I wondered if I ought to insist on paying for it all myself, but to be honest, having the perfect Christmas was proving to be more expensive than I'd realised.

Not only that, but the only trees left were the ones that nobody could afford.

'You're being ever so understanding,' I said as we toured yet another garden centre.

'Oh well. I know how important it is to you.' She looked away. 'Why don't we get that one? It's small, but it's in a pot so we can keep it and use it next year too.'

The tree that she pointed out was two feet tall. It was bushy, but not too bushy at the bottom, tapering up to the ideal seat for an angel. There was no chance it would outgrow the ceiling any time soon, and it would also make the few decorations I'd managed to create look deliberately minimalist, but...

'If we use it every year that'll make it *extra* traditional,' she put in before I could object. 'And I've got some tinsel in my room that would look just perfect... please?'

I'd almost overlooked that it was her Christmas too. 'Of course,' I agreed.

Back home, I positioned our tree in the lounge, then hesitated. Did Rachel want to help decorate it?

'Rach?' I tapped on her door before barging in. 'Do you—?'

She swung round guiltily. 'I was just getting this,' she held up a string of tinsel.

Behind her, on the floor of her wardrobe, was her own secret grotto. There was a tiny tree with sparkly lights, tinsel to spare, and to top it all off, Santa's express *choo-chooed* around the base.

'I... needed to have something Christmassy,' she said weakly.

I realised suddenly, how lucky I was to have a friend who would not only give me the space to find my perfect Christmas, but planned to stay with me through next Christmas too.

'It's the height of naff-ness,' I pointed to the train. 'My mother would love it.'

She giggled, so did I, and a tension that I'd been trying to ignore dissolved between us.

'I'm sorry,' I said. 'Have I been a real pain?'

'Not completely,' she replied. 'Your mum said to let you get it out of your system.'

'You spoke to my mum about this!'

She shrugged, unrepentant. 'She said you get like this every few years, and to remind you of the time you tried to fake Santa's footprints through the lounge.'

'Ah.' Maybe I'd leave that bag of flour in the cupboard after all. 'The twins loved it.'

'She said your dad's work-boots were never the same again.'

I giggled. 'They nicknamed him 'twinkle-toes' after that. Come on, let's stick some carols on, decorate the tree and start on the mince pies.'

The mulled wine was lovely. The mince pies, however, weren't quite right.

'Are you sure that was what that machine was for?' she asked.

'Well, I always get confused between mince and mincemeat, but the shop was so posh I didn't like to ask.'

'Here,' she pulled a couple of shop-bought packets from an end cupboard. 'I got these on offer, buy-one-get-one-free!'

I switched the oven back on to warm them up. 'There's my homemade Christmas cake too.'

'Hmm,' said Rachel. 'I saw how much brandy you put in that. We've put a lot of effort into this Christmas, and I don't intend to miss it!'

© Aug 2017

First published in *My Weekly* Dec 2017

Written next to the pool, in France, on a hot summer morning. You've got to write Christmas stories well in advance. I still have fond memories of waking up an hour before everyone else and writing by the pool. It took me a while to realise it was because France is an hour ahead of the UK, rather than due to any saintliness on my part.

ALL HALLOWS' EVE

'Don't stand there, Florrie. It's not safe.'

I swung round. The complaint of the rotten floorboard beneath my feet suggested that this was good advice, and I took a step back from the window.

'Who are you? How do you know my name?' I'd never seen him before. 'Do you live here?'

The Thackeray house had been empty for years. Every now and then someone would try to do something with it, but it never worked out. Maybe this guy was the latest to try, and perhaps he might achieve where the others had failed because in a weird way, he matched the house. Someone you wouldn't look at twice if it weren't for that desolate look about him, as if he hadn't spoken to a soul in years.

'So many questions. Just like your mother.' He moved forward and peered into my face. 'She had a habit of being places she shouldn't too.'

'I didn't—' I thought about the bag of flour and the fake slime in my rucksack. Probably not the right moment to own up to my fantastic scheme of planting a couple of booby traps to freak out the trick or treaters. Instead, I continued the bizarre conversation with this ragged man, haunting the shadows 'How do you know who I am?'

He shrugged, a hitch of the shoulder that rang a bell from somewhere, and stared out of the window. 'Never knew your father, did you, girl?'

'What—?'

'Know how they met?'

'My mum and dad? He saved her life when she would have fallen. What business is that of yours?'

But he waved me to silence as we both heard a creak on the stair.

A shadow detached itself from the doorway and went to kneel by the window, much as I had. I caught the glint of red hair in the moonlight and recognised Jonas Michaels from my English class.

'Don't stand there,' I repeated the words automatically. 'It's not safe.'

Jonas peered into the darkness around me. 'Who's that?'

I moved forward into the moonlight.

'Oh, hey Florrie,' he walked toward me. 'Same idea?' He grinned and hefted his bag. I flushed, glancing back guiltily at my ragged companion, but he'd vanished.

'Where did he go—?'

But I was interrupted by the splintering of the window behind Jonas, and the howls and catcalls of voices that I definitely recognised as boys from year 9. Their first flour-gunk-and-who-knew-what-else bomb that had taken out the window was followed by a storm of others, and we watched open-mouthed as some of them caught the old chandelier that Jonas had been standing beneath a moment ago. The weakened fittings couldn't take the assault and crashed to the floor, taking the rotten floorboards with it to the room below.

Jonas stared at me in shock. 'How did you know?'

I shrugged helplessly. A hitch of the shoulder that Mum said I'd somehow inherited from the father I'd never known.

© 2017

I decided to include a couple of ghost stories in this collection. They teeter on the cusp between this collection of contemporary stories and my other collection of sci-fi and fantasy stories (which I plan to publish after this one), but I decided they sit ever-so-slightly more comfortably with stories from the real world.

QUIET NEIGHBOURS

Young Martha was already there when Old Martha materialised next to their gravestones, on the plot they'd shared for the last two hundred years.

Old Martha sighed. One of these nights it would be nice to get the space to herself.

The bright moonlight that highlighted the craggy bark of the nearby Elder tree, shone straight through the little girl as she peered towards the newly turned earth of a grave a few plots over.

'Still waiting to see what the new resident is like? He may not show, and even if he does, he might be too modern to understand what you say.' Old Martha couldn't resist a dig, 'I know I don't at times.'

'Anybody would be a change of scenery from you,' retorted Young Martha.

'Careful with that viper tongue of yours, sister dear. Perhaps that's what's emptying the graveyard.' They had seen fewer and fewer of their neighbouring ghosts in recent weeks.

'Maybe they got fed up with you. Lord knows I am after sharing a grave for two hundred years.'

'More likely it's your immaturity. It wears after a century or so.'

'Not half as much as your— where *have* they all gone?' Young Martha interrupted herself. 'Maybe it's something to do with Judgement Day?'

'Isn't that supposed to be much more immediate? There's as much chance of it being those ghosthunters.'

'Them,' snorted Young Martha. 'They wouldn't recognise a full-blown apparition if it tapped them on the nose.'

'Well, something's going on. The ghosts in this graveyard are definitely disappearing.'

'In some cases,' Young Martha gave her a sideways look. 'That wouldn't be such a bad thing.'

'In some cases,' Old Martha looked darkly at the younger. 'You could be right.'

Young Martha chose to ignore that remark, turning back towards the new grave instead. 'There, did you see that? He is coming. I had a feeling if he came at all it would be tonight.'

'You say that every night,' the older woman said mildly. But this time Young Martha was right.

At first it looked as if the wind was stirring the flowers a little, the bright wreath a stark contrast to the few amber leaves that had drifted to the ground nearby. But then a mist arose and gradually coalesced into a figure until finally, a man stood with his back to them, rubbing his head in a clearly puzzled manner.

The two women waited, patiently at first, but soon Young Martha began to fidget.

'How long is he going to stand there? What does he think he's looking at?'

'Quietly now, it can be a shock the first time.'

The younger girl ignored her, 'Excuse me? Hello!'

He swung round and cried out in terror at the sight of them. 'What are you? Where am I? What happened?'

'Not all this again,' muttered the old woman. 'I'd forgotten this bit.'

'You've passed on,' explained the younger girl taking pity on him. 'You'll get used to it after a while, just try to stay calm. What's your name?'

'David.'

'Hello David, do you have any little girls who might visit?'

'Do excuse her manners,' inserted Old Martha. 'She didn't live long enough to learn them properly.'

'At least I didn't outlive my usefulness.'

'Hush child, he doesn't need to hear your prattle.'

David had sunk to his knees on the mound of earth. 'What happened?' he asked again.

'We were hoping you might tell us that.'

He shook his head, 'I don't remember anything.'

'It's like that sometimes. If it was sudden, you wouldn't have any reason to know ahead of time. You may find out from your gravestone when you get it.'

He looked around. 'When do I get my gravestone?'

'Not for another six months,' Old Martha advised. 'The ground needs to settle.'

He sighed, 'Six months till I find out what happened.'

'If then,' she cautioned. 'Some people just never find out.'

'What about you then? Do you know?'

Young Martha straightened her shoulders and stood like a child about to recite. 'My name is Martha Mary Redstone. I was born in 1722, the eldest beloved daughter of Jocelyn and Martin Redstone, sister to Barnabas. I died tragically in 1729 at the age of seven after a sudden illness.'

'I'm so sorry.' He looked over to Old Martha, 'Then you must be her mother?'

'Heaven forbid!' she looked horrified at the thought. 'I was born in 1730. Named Martha Jocelyn Redstone. Eldest surviving daughter of Jocelyn and Martin Redstone, sister to Barnabas and Flora.'

'I'm very confused.'

'It's not difficult,' Young Martha said sourly. 'Not only did she steal my name, she couldn't even manage to get married, so skinflint Barnabas made use of a ready-made grave plot.'

The older Martha rolled her eyes, 'If I'd known what I was setting myself up for I'd have married Jessamy Tucker after all.'

'Let me get this straight,' said David. 'You're sisters, but you have the same name?'

Yes,' explained Old Martha. 'I was born a year after she died. It was traditional to use the same name.'

'And because you never married, you were buried in the same grave?'

'Correct,' she said. 'I think it was tradition rather than parsimony, but you never could tell with our brother Barnaby.'

'I've never heard of that.'

'We did get our own headstones.' Young Martha pointed them out, her smaller stone set slightly in front of Old Martha's larger one.

'Oh.' He looked around the silent graveyard. 'What about the people in all these other graves?'

'Sometimes they're here and sometimes they're not. Some of them never show, we don't know why,' said Old Martha.

'Where are they now?'

'We don't know. All the ghosts have been gradually disappearing over the last month. We were hoping you might know something.'

Young Martha raised her head, 'What was that noise?'

In the silence that followed, they all heard the crunch of footsteps on the gravel pathway.

'What is it?' asked David.

'Shh.' Both Marthas listened intently, then Old Martha turned to him. 'You need to fade.'

'What do you mean?'

'Ghosthunters. They're generally rubbish, but this lot seem to think they're something special, so it's best to keep as low a profile as possible.'

'How?'

'I've never really had to explain it before.' She turned to Young Martha.

'You look too bright,' said the younger girl. 'Think about silence.'

Confused and starting to panic, David closed his eyes and hunched his shoulders. But he was still as clear as day.

'No, no. Not like that,' said Old Martha. 'Like this.'

He watched as she faded out, then tried again, the strain showing on his face.

'Try to relax,' advised Young Martha. He gave her an exasperated look.

The footsteps came closer.

'Hurry,' said Old Martha.

'I can't.' he looked at them helplessly.

Confined to their own grave plot, the Marthas were unable to help when three men rounded the corner of the church and spotted David, highlighted by the full moon.

The two women faded into near invisibility and watched.

David, watching as they faded, finally got the idea and started to grow hazier. But it was too late; the ghosthunters had spread out and were pointing metal boxes in his direction.

The sisters clung together as with a single shouted order the three men simultaneously pressed buttons. A bolt of power surged from each box through the air to David, who gave a howl of terror.

There was a crackle of discharge and then silence.

After a lot of excited chatter, the ghosthunters packed up their equipment and left.

Both Marthas realised they were still clutching each other's hands and moved apart.

'What happened? What was that... thing?' asked Young Martha in a tiny voice.

'I don't know.'

'Is he... gone?'

'I think so.'

They were silent for some time. Finally Young Martha stirred, 'I think perhaps sharing a grave is not so bad after all.'

The older woman smiled at her sister, 'No, not so bad.'

First published in a collection for Chudleigh Writer's Circle Dec 2015.

Second published on my blog, www.angelawooldridge.wordpress.com in Oct 2016 as part of a storytime blog-hop.

The inspiration for this came from a visit to Chudleigh church which included a tour of the graveyard. I was particularly struck by one of the graves which not only had a normal sized headstone, but also a much smaller one in front of it. Both held the same name.

I learned that back when people often lost their children at an early age, they would re-use the name (often a family name) for the next child, and that child would then be buried in the same grave. (Not until they'd died though!)

PATSY

'Good morning ladies!'

Concentrating on tying her belt correctly, Patsy hadn't noticed the man breezing past the candidates waiting to enter the examination hall.

She glanced up and froze, her stomach dropping to the region of her knees. She tightened her belt in an attempt to squeeze out the sudden hollow feeling there. It was two years since she'd last seen Nick Farrell, but now the utter mortification of their last meeting came flooding back. She'd been unlucky yes, but to top that she'd been stupid too.

It had been her first karate grading, for yellow belt. A nerve-wracking event for anyone and the examining instructor was a real mean bastard. Even so, once she began, she felt her usual elation at performing each stance, each technique, correctly. The thrill of moving in unison with everyone else, '… snapping ball kick, left side blade, front crossover and out…' back and forth across the hall, '..upwards block, right handsword, and freeze there, DO NOT pull back…'

The man was an absolute tyrant, but it kept her on her toes, back straight, elbows up, please don't let me screw anything up. The sweat streamed down her face and she thought longingly of the towel and water bottle in her bag.

'What was my last instruction..?'

Dammit, her only lapse of concentration had been picked up by the examiner. 'Er…'

'So, we have someone who doesn't need to listen to instructions. Perhaps the force is so strong that you don't have to, hmm?'

'No …sir.' She wilted, wishing herself elsewhere.

' 'No Mr Farrell!' don't you know the correct form of address? What's your name?'

'Patsy sir... uh Mr Farrell.' She could feel everyone else in the room standing in painful silence, eyes averted, grateful not to be in her place.

'Patsy, huh? D'you know what a patsy is?'

Oh God.

'Someone set up for a fall. Is that you, *Patsy*?'

Stop now, please.

'Let that be a lesson to everyone, if you don't pay attention you're setting yourself up for a fall. Now, techniques and some sparring.' He moved on.

Swine. She gritted her teeth and continued, her earlier elation gone. If only the ground would swallow her or someone would break her leg, then she could leave.

But he hadn't finished with her yet. 'Do you know what these are?'

'Nunchuks, Mr Farrell.' *Dammit, leave me alone.*

'And what do we use nunchucks for?'

'Uh... I've... uh, not had the opportunity to use them... Mr Farrell...'

'Well then Patsy, it's about time you did. Hold this, no like that! Now, upwards block, inward block. Does everyone see how the standard defence suddenly becomes an attack with a weapon in your hand?' He took her through the whole five-star block set, stumbling, halting. Stuff that she *knew*, but here in front of everyone, her mind went blank and all she could think about was how much longer this ordeal was going to last.

By some miracle she passed the grading, but turned down the offer of drinks with her usual class. She just wanted to shower off her shame and go home.

But there was Mr *bloody* Farrell again. She tried to slink past, but he came right up to her. 'Patsy! I'm so glad I saw you!' She glanced around, desperate to escape, but there was no-one in sight.

'I hope you can forgive my using you as an example. I only use people who obviously have the strength of character to take it. It keeps everyone on their toes, and some of the others,' he smiled winningly at her, 'need that little boost to bring themselves up to the mark.'

'I'm not sure—'

'Let me buy you a drink so I can make amends, hmm?'

'Oh I don't think—'

'And to reassure me that you don't take it personally?'

In jeans, smiling disarmingly at her, he just didn't seem to be the same person who'd ripped her to shreds an hour ago.

'Do you have a twin brother?' she asked suspiciously.

He laughed and picked up her bag. 'C'mon, I know this great place round the corner.' With her bag taken hostage she could only follow, and hope she wouldn't meet anyone she knew.

Over the next couple of hours he was transformed into a charming, pleasant companion. The wine probably helped. 'Oh no – not water, you need something bubbly to celebrate your first successful martial arts grading!' So while her dehydrated body craved pints of cold, pure water, instead she drank glasses of sweet fizz that hummed through her bloodstream and set her already flushed face aglow.

He spoke of how much he admired women in the sport; '…Women have a more natural fluidity with the forms…' and of competitions; 'Of course, the world championships are in Vegas.' And somewhere in that rosy haze he grew more likeable, more attractive, and although never completely sure how, she found herself spending the afternoon tangled in his bedsheets.

A few days later, past the heady euphoria of success and sex, and starting to feel a bit soiled by the experience, she paused on entering her karate class.

'So, did Nick Farrell get up to his usual tricks again?' someone asked her instructor.

She went cold.

'I gather he made his one of his usual conquests, but didn't manage to remember her name. He did rake poor Patsy here over the coals though.' He waved her over. 'Well done for surviving your ordeal!'

Now, two years and four belt grades later, their paths had finally crossed again.

'Are you ok?'

Patsy surfaced from her funk and realised that her friend, Debbie, had been talking for a while.

'Yes, fine.' Thank God he hadn't recognised her.

'...After the way he treated me at the grading. But he seemed so nice and complimentary, 'a natural fluidity with the forms,' he said. Apparently that's one of his favourite chat up lines. Quite a club I turned out to belong to. Arrogant sod. And then he just pretends not to know you after that!'

A slow burning ember ignited in her midriff as Debbie's words sank in. *How dare he! How dare he!* She clenched her fists, her nails digging into her palms. Oh, how she wanted to hit something. Someone! But this was not the time or place. Her green belt grading was far more important than some complete arsewipe who couldn't keep his trousers zipped.

That fury continued to roil inside her as the session began, so she used the aggression to fuel her moves. Snapping *kick*, reverse *thrust*, hammer *punch*. Her concentration was so intense that she almost missed her moment.

Noticing her focus, Nick pounced on the chance to show someone up. But she was calmer now, not the naïve beginner she had once been.

'What's your name?'

'Patricia, Mr Farrell,' she replied.

He moved on. Despite a regret that she hadn't been able to flay him with the acid remarks that now popped into her head, she was relieved that the moment had passed with her self-respect intact. She caught a glance of approval from her own instructor across the room.

But, dissatisfied with his earlier failure, Nick picked on her as an example while they were working through their forms.

'So, as one of the ladies among us, how do you think the forms contribute to self defence?'

She took a deep breath, trying to contain her resentment. 'I've heard that women have a more natural fluidity with the forms.' There were a couple of gasps from nearby. 'That may suggest why certain moves come more naturally to us, such as the reverse elbow.' She demonstrated with a forceful elbow into his midriff, leaving him hunched forward and gasping. 'And of course the old favourite.' She turned and grabbed his shoulders, bringing her knee up and fully expecting to come into contact with the hard plastic of his protective box. But she was completely unprepared when he collapsed to the floor, retching and moaning.

There was a stunned silence broken by a couple of smothered sniggers.

She was saved by her instructor. Rapidly gesturing for someone to remove Nick, he came over to her. 'Thank you, ah... Patricia, for your excellent example of how the simplest moves can be the most effective... and to Mr Farrell for reminding us all of the importance of remembering our protective clothing!'

I wrote this on the first creative writing course I took with teacher, friend and novelist, Cathie Hartigan. At first, it was about ballroom dancing until it dawned on me, as I researched dance steps on the internet, that if I used karate instead it'd save a lot of time and I'd know what I was talking about.

ABOUT THE AUTHOR

Angela Wooldridge lives in Devon, in a rackety old house with her husband and the railway children.

She always wanted to be a writer, ever since the early days of exploring Narnia with the Pevensies and eating sardine sandwiches with the Famous Five.

Her stories have appeared in magazines such as My Weekly and The People's Friend, in anthologies and been shortlisted in various competitions.

You can read her blog at www.angelawooldridge.wordpress.com.

Or follow her on Twitter: @angwooldridge

ACKNOWLEDGEMENT

I'd always wanted to write, ever since I was a kid and used to read my stories to my English teacher (poor chap). But it was years before I took my first creative writing class, which was such a game-changer. It's thanks to my husband, Tony, for encouraging me to do so; The first class was on his birthday and our youngest, at ten months, had just pulled himself along Tony's jeans to plant his face in coffee cake. I had to leave him clearing up the mess as I dashed out the door. That writing tutor was Cathie Hartigan, now a fellow Exeter Writer and friend. I always felt that those first classes were like turning an old unused tap. Stiff at first, and to start with, some rusty, sludgy stuff came out, but that rapidly became a flood. And now? Now my stream of words have finally found their way to the Amazon river ;) So thanks to everyone at Exeter Writers for their friendship and support. To Jenny Kane for her lovely advice and guidance. To Dianne Bown-Wilson for giving up her time to proofread.

And, of course, most of all to Tony; for sharing his cake, cleaning up the kids, and giving me the time, space and support to write.

Printed in Great Britain
by Amazon